F. Carruthers Gould

The elector's picture book

F. Carruthers Gould

The elector's picture book

ISBN/EAN: 9783741193316

Manufactured in Europe, USA, Canada, Australia, Japa

Cover: Foto ©Andreas Hilbeck / pixelio.de

Manufactured and distributed by brebook publishing software
(www.brebook.com)

F. Carruthers Gould

The elector's picture book

THE ELECTOR'S PICTURE BOOK

WITH

SCENES AND FACES IN PARLIAMENT, 1886–1892.

Pall Mall Gazette "Extra"—No. 63.

JUNE 1892.
[Price ONE SHILLING.

BUCKLING ON HIS ARMOUR.

(With Apologies to HABLOT BROWNE in *Barnaby Rudge.*

THE POLICY OF NEGATION.

"A man who is to give an entertainment might as well send word to every house in the neighbourhood and ask for the bones, the waste, the refuse, and the washings, and put them together and serve them up to his guests as the banquet on which they were to feed."—(Mr. GLADSTONE, of Tory policy: House of Commons, *May* 24.)

THE NEWCASTLE PROGRAMME.

1. Home Rule for Ireland.
2. More Home Rule for London.
3. Welsh Disestablishment.
4. One Man One Vote. Registration Reform. Payment of Members.
5. Popular Control for Public Elementary Schools.
6. Village Councils.
7. Thorough Land Reform. Taxation of Ground-rents. Compensation for Disturbance and Improvements.

8. Local Option.
9. Scotch Disestablishment.
10. Equalisation of Death Duties.
11. Division of Rates between Owner and Occupier.
12. Taxation of Mining Royalties.
13. Free Breakfast Table.
14. Extension of Factory Acts.
15. Mending or Ending of House of Lords.

A 2

II.—*THE TWO IRISH POLICIES.*

Here we have the two Irish policies illustrated and contrasted in two beautiful cartoons by Mr. HENRY HOLIDAY:—

THE LIBERAL POLICY.

THE TORY POLICY.

III.—MOTHER BALFOURS SYRUP.

Mr. Balfour, having applied Coercion in vain, now tries to see what the Soothing Syrup of Local
Government will do:—

" For he can thoroughly enjoy
The bottle if he pleases."

Lord Salisbury and Mr. Balfour stand shivering on the trapeze, and wondering if the net will stand their
flying leap. Mr. Showman Chamberlain watches anxiously.

The Grand Old Jockey, spick and span, and ready as ever, brings out the favourite, and waits eagerly for the start.

V.—GIVING THE LABOURER A LIFT.

Among his other plans and projects, Mr. Gladstone has found time to give the rural labourer a lift in the world. Speaking to the Conference of Rural Labourers which assembled in London, he pledged himself definitely to obtain Parish Councils, further facilities for Allotments, and other measures for improving the conditions of life in villages. "It is as the complement of your freedom," he said, "that I wish, in the first instance, for Parish Councils; but I wish them also for another reason, which is more material. I feel that the improvement of your material condition is the central and vital object which has most of all brought you here to-day. We see our way to some very important improvements in the condition of the rural population." What is required is "a local authority conversant with the minutest details of space and of local history, and a Parish Council, Parish Assembly—call it what you like—if it is a true and efficient Parish Assembly."

VI.—*A LIVELY CORPSE.*

"Home Rule," according to Mr. Chamberlain, is "as dead as Queen Anne." This shows the result when they tried to nail it down.

VII.—*CUTTING HIM OFF.*

Since the beginning of the year 1886 two great attempts have been made to cut off the Grand Old Leader, and this is how it was done on both occasions :—

VIII.—*THE BY-ELECTIONS.*

Lord Salisbury and the Unionists profess to care very little for by-elections. But, when a man professes not to care for the laws of gravity, it does not matter much to the laws of gravity, but it often matters a great deal to himself; for this is how the laws of gravity assert themselves :—

THE LAW OF GRAVITY.

THE BY-ELECTIONS (continued).

Lord Salisbury has been badly bruised by falling apples since 1886, as this little table will show :—

LIBERAL GAINS.	TORY GAINS.
1. Burnley.	Doncaster.
2. Spalding.	
3. Coventry.	
4. Northwich.	
5. Edinburgh W.	
6. Southampton.	
7. Govan.	
8. Kennington.	
9. Rochester.	
10. North Bucks.	
11. Peterborough.	
12. St. Pancras.	
13. Carnarvon District.	
14. Barrow.	
15. Eccles.	
16. Hartlepool.	
17. Harborough.	
18. Stowmarket.	
19. Wisbeach.	
20. South Molton.	
21. Rossendale.	

In 1886 the Unionist majority in the House of Commons was 118. In 1892 it had declined, owing to the above elections and to conversions within the House, to 66. This is how certain people were affected by the results :—

"SYMPATHY." (With Apologies to Mr. Briton Rivière, R.A.)

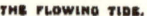

THE FLOWING TIDE.

A CHANGE OF AYR.

HOW THEY TOOK IT.

THE BY-ELECTIONS (continued).

"NO COMPENSATION" WINS. -(Southampton.)   THE PIGOTTISTS LEAVE THE FIELD. -(Kennington.)

THE CENTRE OF GRAVITY.

"Sir Henry James says that the Unionists are the centre of gravity of the political world. Well, that is "a very important situation. It must be a great thing to be a centre of gravity. In the religion of the Hindoos they believe that the world rests on an elephant, but there was the difficulty as to whom the elephant rested on. It rested on the tortoise; the tortoise rested on nothing; and so the elephant of the Tory party rests on the tortoise of the Liberal Unionists, and the Liberal Unionists rest on nothing. Well, gentlemen, the policy of the Government is the policy of the tortoise. No, I beg the tortoise's pardon, it is a silent animal."—(Sir WILLIAM HARCOURT, at Derby, *February 1888.*)

IX.—"*MEND OR END?*"

But, say the Unionists, "it won't matter a bit if all the elections go against us. We can fall back on the House of Lords." That is a very old threat, and no one knows better how to meet it than the Grand Old Boxer:—

"Lord Salisbury, in a speech some two or three months back, contemplated the possibility—his mind is open to that extent —of a Liberal victory at the General Election. He contemplated the passing of a Home Rule Bill through the House of Commons, but he assured his friends that all would not then be over, for they might still rely upon—I am quoting the sacred words—upon the play of the other parts of the Constitution. Strip off the disguise from these words. There is but one other part of the Constitution that could possibly perform such a prank as to interpose itself between the deliberate judgment of the nation and the incorporation of that judgment in the form of law, and that is the House of Lords. I hope—nay, more, I believe—that the House of Lords will not accept the deplorable suggestion tendered to them by the Prime Minister. I believe that they will decline to let their position in the Constitution be used for so ruinous a purpose. But this I know well, that if they should be reduced to a policy so unfortunate, they themselves will be the first to repent of it. They will raise up a question which will take precedence of every other question, because upon that alone would depend whether this country was or was not a self-governing country, or whether, on the contrary, there was a power, not upon the throne or behind the throne, but between the throne and the people, that would stop altogether the action of a constitutional machine, now, as we trust, if not perfected, yet being brought nearer to perfection, by the labour, the struggles, the patriotism, and the wisdom of many generations."—(Mr. GLADSTONE, at Newcastle, *October* 2, 1891.)

X.—MR. GLADSTONE'S DREAM.

The opening of the campaign was fixed for the morrow, and Mr. Gladstone had tucked himself into the corner of a first-class carriage on his way from Euston to Midlothian. Tired with many days of thought and preparation, he quickly closed his eyes. Then a strange thing happened. Faces began to appear in the windows, and two white-robed figures stood before the sleeper. The first bore scales in her hands, and looked neither to the right nor to the left. The second was like unto her in dignity, but was winged beneath her robes, and carried a wreath in her hand. For a moment the aspect of the strange visitors became strangely familiar. Their faces mingled into one, and passed into such marble similitude as one may see on an abbey wall where some great statesman's effigy seems still to be bidding his countrymen to be just and fear not, and to set the captives free. But the marble melted again in an instant, and the two figures, resuming their separate forms, declared their names. "I am Justice," said the first; "And I am Freedom," said the second; "follow us."

No sooner had the word been said than the railway carriage was transformed into the parlour of a poor dwelling, filled with a workman's family preparing to eat their frugal meal. It was like the Cratchits' Christmas party, Mr. Gladstone thought. Like the heroes of the Christmas Carol, they were not a handsome family, not well dressed, and not well off. But there was plenty to eat, and the cheapness of all their substantial fare was the theme of universal admiration. They were happy, grateful, pleased with one another, and contented with the time.

They did not see their visitors, and Mr. Gladstone, fearing to interrupt their cheerful seclusion, turned to go. But before his guides suffered him to depart she that carried the scales in her hand pointed to piles of tariff items in one of them, and showed him how "Gladstone's Budgets" in the other had made them kick the beam, and, as she did so, the scene changed again, and the floor was strewn with newspapers and books—no longer the luxuries only of the rich, but the common possessions of every citizen. Mr. Gladstone had his Dante running in his brain, and remembered how the favourite poet had preached the doctrine of "Volgar Eloquence," and the duty of the learned and wise to share their treasures with the unlearned multitude. He remembered, too, all the words of simple eloquence in which his old friend, John Bright, had in other days praised the civilising mission of the penny press, and, as he remembered, he was glad. And Justice once more took him by the hand, and was showing him "Gladstone's abolition of the paper duties" prevailing against the interests of the "classes," when the scene changed, and he was carried from the reading-room to the open fields. Here were labourers discussing, when their work was done, the issues of the common weal. The intelligence of an enfranchised people shone in their eyes, and the self-respect of responsible citizens was apparent in their bearing. "Hark," said Justice, "it is 'Gladstone's next great blow for right' that they are discussing." Mr. Gladstone turned to hear, but, as he did so, they were no longer English labourers, who stood before him, but their colonial brothers. Signs of peace and prosperity were on every side; and the colonists, fresh from the conduct of their own affairs, were pledging the Queen, their brethren at home, and the common country of them all. Mr. Gladstone inquired of his guides what this community might be. "It is Gladstone town," was the answer; "for in the far North-West they have named their home by the name that

MR. GLADSTONES DREAM (continued).

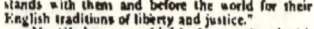

stands with them and before the world for their English traditions of liberty and justice."

Mr. Gladstone would fain have parleyed with this friendly folk, but his guides dissuaded him. "We have other things to see," they said, and Justice, who had till now been walking linked with Freedom at Mr. Gladstone's side, changed her place and gave way to Freedom. And Freedom bade him look again, and lo! he saw a row of Eastern peasants, men and women, tied each to a stake. A band of ruffians, with cruelty and lust stamped upon their faces, were approaching to work their foul will upon their victims, and behind the ruffians stood a grim figure, in English dress, alternately encouraging them on and shutting one eye, so as to pretend he could not see. Nearer and nearer drew the fiends of lust and murder; and advancing ever in step with them went the representative of the English race. "It is infamous,"

cried Mr. Gladstone, as he looked upon the scene, "that such things should be, and intolerable if they must be that any man who speaks the English tongue should consent thereto." "Thou hast said it," replied his guide, and, as she spoke, the sinister figure vanished into thin air, and Mr. Gladstone saw himself holding a banner aloft in a vacant place, and on the banner were the words "Bulgarian Atrocities." A strange light gleamed in Mr. Gladstone's eyes, and he looked as one about to buckle on his armour to refight the battles of his prime. "Stay," said his guide, and, as she spoke, the scene was changed again, this time to Italian soil, and Mr. Gladstone saw Freedom spread her wings and enter a dark dungeon, kept by a crowned and sworded sentinel, where a venerable prisoner, whose mild eyes and lofty brow proclaimed a blameless life of public good, lay in heavy chains. And, as Justice entered, the warder trembled and the chains relaxed. Mr. Gladstone looked and looked again, and behold! the prison cell was empty, and by the open door were the pages of a book inscribed with the words, "Letters to the Earl of Aberdeen"; the words caught Mr. Gladstone's eye, and he stooped to read the full legend, but Justice bade him look up once more, and, instead of an Italian dungeon, he saw an Irish landscape with a deadly tree in the midst. Two of its branches were fresh lopped off, and Mr. Gladstone smiled as he saw that the woodman's axe was of the Hawarden make. But a third and deadlier branch remained. Its form stood out in ghastly

hardness against the sky, and seemed like the line of some grim castle's battlements. Beneath its cruel shade were men and women, some in chains and some in rags, and all with marks of suffering or indignation upon their faces. And, as his guides bade Mr. Gladstone look, he heard a voice sounding in his ears with a message that he remembered to have read in some ancient legend. "It is the voice of the Irish," he said, "the voice of those who live near the wood

of Fochlad, which is near the western sea, and thus they cry: 'We pray thee, old man, to come and henceforward walk among us.'" And, as he repeated the message, Freedom and Justice took him by the hand and led him to a point of vantage, whence he saw a figure, with a face that he knew, but clad in the garb of a saint and hero of old, driving a herd of evil creatures into the sea. "It is a call, then, for a new St. Patrick," Mr. Gladstone cried, and started to his feet to find himself in Edinburgh Station, and a vast crowd waiting to welcome him for the last great fight.

Mr. Balfour has played many parts since the Tory Government came into power. Just now we saw him as a nurse endeavouring to administer his patent soothing syrup to the Irish infant. Here we have three pictures of him drawn respectively by a Conservative, a Liberal, and an Irish Nationalist:—

PARADISO + PURGATORIO + INFERNO

This is the work of the late Mr. W. H. Smith, and represents Mr. Balfour as a canonised saint. "I have never known nerve and decision so admirably united with judgment and with courage; I have never known those qualities so conspicuously guided and directed by discretion and tact. ... Mr. Balfour has devoted himself to work, which, take it as you like, cannot be otherwise than distasteful work—a work which falls upon a man as a matter of duty, and not by any means as a matter of choice."—(Mr. Smith, at the Primrose League, April 18, 1888.)

This is the work of Mr. John Morley, and represents Mr. Balfour as a superior being who "treats the Irish Members with the easy contempt of a white man for the negroes of a cotton plantation." "I do not like to think this is a good picture. I do not like to think of the chief governor of a country in its distraction and confused state being like the Epicurean gods of the old world. You remember the lines in which the Poet Laureate has described those old gods, how they smiled in secret, looking over wasted lands," &c.—(Mr. John Morley, at Blackburn, April 18, 1888.)

This is the work of Mr. T. P. O'Connor, and represents Mr. Balfour as the cock-a-hoop secretary. "Mr. Balfour had complained of being called a Nero and a Cromwell, but he called him a profound and unutterable cad. He was a whimpering creature, who, with a perfumed handkerchief, played with the blood of his fellow-men, and rejoiced at the misfortunes and sufferings of the Irish people."—(Mr. T. P. O'Connor, Liverpool, April 15, 1888.)

MR. BALFOUR, THE COERCIONIST (continued).

We do not hear much about Coercion as a General Election comes on, but this is what Coercion was a very few years ago. Readers of *Barnaby Rudge* will remember the gaoler, and here is Mr. Balfour as gaoler :—

"You've had law," he said, crossing his legs and elevating his eyebrows ; "laws have been made a purpose for you ; a very handsome prison's been made a purpose for you ; a parson's kept a purpose for you ; a constitutional officer's appointed a purpose for you ; carts is maintained a purpose for you—and yet you're not contented ! Will you hold your noise ? Yes, sir, in the furthest ?"

MR. BALFOUR, THE COERCIONIST (*continued*).

Then we have Mr. Balfour as spider extending his web across the Irish Channel and catching the Irish flies at Westminster as well as in Dublin. (During 1888 several Members were arrested in England, and one was served with a writ actually in the precincts of the House of Commons.)

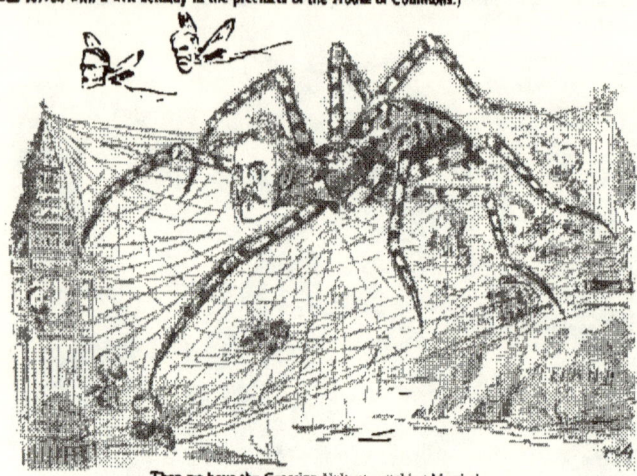

Then we have the Coercion Vulture watching his victim :—

MR. BALFOUR, THE COERCIONIST (continued).

Next we get Mr. Balfour as executioner, a rôle which received the special patronage of Lord Salisbury :—

"Let us assume that these gentlemen are what are called political offenders. . . . I will not go very far back 100 or 130 years ago, political offenders well their heads appeared along Temple Bar, I think. But we need not go so far back as that. Let us take the case of India—that was only thirty years ago. In 1857, if there was a political movement it was the movement that is known as the Indian Mutiny ; but I do not think any particular delicacy was shown in punishing the offenders on that occasion. My impression is that most of them were blown from the mouth of guns."—(Lord SALISBURY, at Edinburgh, *December* 1888.)

R. I. C.
A PROMISING RECRUIT

Smashing the dial because the shadow won't go back. "The National League is dead," said Mr. Balfour and his friends, but, like Home Rule, it proved a very lively corpse.

MR. BALFOUR, THE COERCIONIST (continued).

Lord Salisbury, as is well known, has a turn for scientific and mechanical pursuits. Mr. Balfour's rule in Ireland was famous, among other things, for the use in evictions of an improved kind of battering-ram, christened by an affectionate peasantry " Balfour's Maiden." It is whispered that Uncle and Nephew spent their holidays in the laboratory at Hatfield devising this pretty instrument of resolute government.

" BALFOUR'S MAIDEN."

MR. BALFOUR, THE COERCIONIST (continued).

Mr. Balfour's unique achievement as a Coercionist was to deprive his prisoners of their clothes. Here he is running off with Mr. O'Brien's breeches : -

"THE RAPE OF O'BRIEN'S BREECHES"

This is what it might come to some day if the situation was reversed :

MR. BALFOUR, THE COERCIONIST (continued).

But Mr. Balfour declared it was very good for them ; they actually increased in weight ·

And not only did he make them change their clothes, but he cut their hair and beards, and was ready to do the same for all his opponents in the House of Commons :--

MR. BALFOUR, THE COERCIONIST (continued).

So the evictions went on merrily with Mr. Balfour's assistance. He was a vigilant gaoler; he told his men " not to hesitate to shoot " ; and, when he couldn't prosecute the Irishmen in any other way, he hunted up a Statute of Edward III. :—

THE CROWBAR BRIGADE AT WORK

ONE OF THE "CRIMINALS"

TRIUMPH FOR THE BRITISH
FLAG.

HOMELESS

SHADOWING.

MR. BALFOUR, THE COERCIONIST (continued).

Mr. Balfour, however, gloried in it all, and glories still. He was not half so proud, he said, of the Local Government Bill as of Coercion. It is as the Coercionist—as "Bomba Balfour"—that he elects to be remembered. So, by way of closing this chapter, we give a design for the Unionist Arms, and another for a Balfour Medal :—

THE UNIONIST ARMS.

The Coat is thus blazoned :—Dexter chief, one gaol window barry of six. Sinister, vert gutty de sang, one pair handcuffs, one bowl skilly. On a fess sable one plank bed. Base, sanguine semée de bayonets, two resident removable magistrates blatant improper. Crest : A. Balfour rampant errerant. In dexter hand, a Coercion Act ; in sinister hand, a trophy. Under feet, promises and pledges torn and trampled. Supporters : Two members of Royal Irish Constabulary combattant. Motto : R.I.C. (said to stand for "Requiescant in Carcere ").

THE BALFOUR MEDAL.

XII.—THE STORY OF PIGOTT.

But some of Mr. Balfour's friends objected to putting Irish Members in prison, and cutting their hair, and stealing their clothes. So some means had to be found of persuading them to vote for the Coercion Bill, and this is how it was done. One day a very crafty pieman called on a certain Simple Simon, who lived in Printing-house Square. Simple Simon happened to be napping just then, but he took the pie, and brought it to his master, who was overjoyed to hear that it contained something that would poison Home Rule and destroy the Home Rule Chief. The pie was opened, and was found to contain a

"SIMPLE SIMON."

letter signed by Mr. C. S. Parnell, who said he was very sorry he had been obliged to condemn the murderers of Phœnix Park. "I will print this in my paper," said the master, "and all the world will see what scoundrels and villains the Irish leaders are." So it was printed on the day when the Coercion-for-ever-and-ever Bill was going to be read a second time in the House of Commons, and all the Unionist Members reading it said, "We must vote for this Bill," and Coercion was passed by a great majority. When the Irish Members declared it was false, they were told that they were liars, and the Government

THE TWO OLD FRIENDS. A GOOD STORY.
(With Apologies to Leo HERMANN.)

refused to appoint a committee to inquire into the matter, and continued to denounce them as murderers and cowards. But the Irish Members persisted, and something had to be done. Then a brilliant idea occurred to someone, and, Simple Simon's master and the head of the Government happening to be "old friends," they met and talked it out. It was a splendid idea, and they chuckled over it immensely and decided to go shares. Old friend Smith and his Government were to provide three judges, and lend old friend Walter their great Attorney to conduct the prosecution. The Attorney

The Times

MONDAY, APRIL 18, 1887.

THE

PHOENIX PARK

MURDERS:

FACSIMILE OF A

LETTER FROM MR. PARNELL,

EXCUSING HIS PUBLIC

CONDEMNATION OF THE CRIME.

THE STORY OF PIGOTT (*continued*).

was to draw up a long list of accusations, and to postpone the letter as long as he liked. So the three judges met, and the Attorney kept talking and calling witnesses who knew about everything,

THE PIGOTT PYRAMID.

How pleased and proud *Delane* would be
These graceful acrobats to see !

THE STORY OF PIGOTT (*continued*).

except about the letter for three long months. At last they came to the letter, and then a much

greater Attorney on the other side took the matter in hand, with the aid of his friends Lewis and

THE COLLAPSE OF THE PYRAMID.

What next those acrobats befell
Gave great enjoyment to Parnell.

THE STORY OF PIGOTT *(continued).*

Labouchere, and the whole fabric came tumbling down. Pigott, the forger, fled and committed suicide, and most pitiable was the fate of the thousand others who had flourished on his calumnies.

" And, behold, the whole herd ran violently down a steep place into the sea and perished in the waters."

THE STORY OF PIGOTT *(continued)*.

A BIRD'S-EYE VIEW OF THE PARNELL COMMISSION.

THE STORY OF PIGOTT (continued).

'But the case of the Attorney whom old friend Smith had lent to old friend Walter was the worst of all. He excused himself by saying that he was really two persons, and that one of his persons was not at all responsible for what the other person did. So one of his persons tried to whitewash the other, and his friends erected a pedestal and put the whitewashed person upon it, and called him St. Webster. And every Unionist declared that what St. Webster did had nothing to do with the Attorney-General or with the Attorney-General's friends in the House of Commons.

THE WHITEWASHING OF " ST, WEBSTER,"

THE STORY OF PIGOTT (continued).

But the final result of it all was that the position of the two parties was reversed. The accusers were the accused:—

"The inquiry intended as a curse has proved to be a blessing. Designed, prominently designed to ruin one man, it has been his vindication. In opening this case I said we represented the accused. My Lords, I claim leave to-day to say that the positions are reversed. We are the accusers; the accused are there."—(Sir CHARLES RUSSELL, in the Special Commission Court, *April 12, 1889*.)

And though the whole Unionist party had used his wares and flourished on them for four years, they left "old friend" Walter to pay the bill:—

PAYING THE BILL.

XIII.—PIGOTTISM-CUM-PARNELLISM.

The Tories have passed through three stages in their treatment of Mr. Parnell. In 1885, when they wanted the Irish vote, they were very polite to him. Lord Salisbury called him the "Irish Chief," and made a speech at Newport which was full of politeness and conciliation. That was the first stage. But the moment Mr. Gladstone had introduced the Home Rule Bill and 'Mr. Parnell had accepted it and was supporting it, they turned completely round and said that he was one of the wickedest men who ever lived, and that if he hadn't actually committed murder he had condoned and encouraged it. Then they produced the forged letter and tried to ruin him that way. Thus, for four years, they abused and persecuted and calumniated him in every way. That was the second stage. Then came the third stage, when Mr. Parnell, found guilty of adultery in the Divorce Court, declined to retire from the leadership of the party. From that moment Mr. Parnell became a hero once more. When the fate of the battle over the Irish leadership was still uncertain, Lord Salisbury gave the Unionist party his "tip." Speaking in Lord Hartington's constituency, he remarked jocularly that no doubt in that sporting county most of them had got bets on the contest for or against Mr.

"TWO TO ONE ON PARNELL, I LAY."

Parnell, and for his part he let it be seen clearly enough which side he meant to back. He said, "It may be a weakness of human nature, but perhaps I prefer the man who is fighting desperately for his life to the crew whom he made and who are turning against him."

The cue was promptly taken. The Tory and Unionist press vied in taunts and misrepresentations in the interests of Mr. Parnell, and against his opponents. Their admiration of his "courage," "resolution," "adroitness," "dignity," and so forth was effusively expressed, while no consideration was left unurged which might terrorise or detract from those who resisted his demands.

What was the explanation of all this sudden weakness of the Pigottists for Mr. Parnell? It was, of course, not that they hated Mr. Parnell less, but that they hated Mr. Gladstone and the cause of Home Rule more. Mr. Parnell's success would have meant the failure of that cause indefinitely. Therefore it was that the *Times* never once ceased, since the nature of the issue became clear, to belaud Mr. Parnell. This is why the man, for whom no accusation or calumny was once bad enough, suddenly became for the *Times* a man "of Napoleonic qualities," for whom the Paper-Unionists have more "respect and sympathy" than for the "crew of Opportunists" opposed to him—a man whose "private character has been subjected to scurrilous attack"—a man "the spell of whose victories lies strung upon his countrymen." This was why the patriotic majority of the Irish party who preferred in the crisis their Cause to their Leader, and who once were taunted by the *Times* with being mere Parnellite "items," afterwards became for the veracious and high-principled paymasters of Pigott "a crew of Opportunists" seeking an occasion "to gratify their personal hatreds," a set of "high-collared respectabilities," whose opposition to Mr. Parnell amounted to "desertion," "treason," and "infamy"

XIV.—" ULSTERIA."

Just as they have mingled Pigottism and Parnellism, so also they have tried to play off Catholics against Protestants and Protestants against Catholics. While applauding the bigotry of the Ulster Orangemen, and raising the "no Popery" cry all over the north they went humbly to the Pope and his envoy, Monsignor  Persico, and begged for their help in putting down the Nationalists of the south. "The Unionists," said Mr. Morley (February 1888), are going about beating the hideous Orange drum in Ulster with one hand, and with the other stealthily plucking at the sleeve of Monsignor Persico."

Then as the Election has come nearer, they have all been seized with a new and terrible complaint called "Ulsteria," which produces the following result :—

VICTIMS OF ULSTERIA. COL. SAUNDERSON, MR. RUSSELL, DUKE OF DEVONSHIRE, AND LORD SALISBURY.

The Ulster argument was not so much an opinion as a disease, and, if he had to choose a name for it, he should choose a word which accurately expressed it, and at the same time by its sound conveyed the idea of a similarity to a malady which sometimes overwhelmed the intellect and obscured the mental faculties of the human race, particularly the weaker portion of it—the name of "Ulsteria." Mr. CAMPBELL-BANNERMANN, at Glasgow, June 7.)

XV.—LORD SALISBURY'S "BLAZERS."

Seven years ago Mr. Goschen declared he would not give a blank cheque to Lord Salisbury. He was a wise man—in those days. For whatever else he can do, Lord Salisbury is quite unable to control his tongue. His speeches are a joy—to his political opponents. As Mr. Morley once said of them, each is sure to contain "at least one blaring indiscretion."

explained this by saying that of course the Liberals did better this time because last time they had a "black man" for a candidate, and you couldn't expect a British constituency to elect a "black man." It so happened that just when Lord Salisbury was having his jibe at this Indian gentlemen, and declaring that no British constituency would elect him,

Here are just a few taken from his speeches of the last six years.

A Parsee gentleman, much esteemed by all who know him, contested Holborn in 1886. Two years later there was a by-election in the same place, and the Tory majority was much reduced. Speaking at Edinburgh a few days afterwards, Lord Salisbury

other "black men," native Princes of India, were most loyally offering to defend the frontiers of the great British dependency.

Black people seem to have a great fascination for Lord Salisbury. A couple of years previously he had compared the Irish people to Hottentots :—

["We are asked to have confidence in the Irish

people. Confidence depends upon the people in whom you are to confide. You would not confide free representative institutions to the Hottentots, for instance."—(St. James' Hall, *May* 16, 1886.)]

Next we come to Lord Salisbury as an anarchist, waving the red flag to Ulster, and encouraging the

Orangemen to "come on" against the Imperial Parliament :—

["Parliaments, like kings, may take a course which, while it is technically within the legal limits of their attribution, is yet entirely at variance and in conflict with the institutions by which they rule. James II. forgot that law, and we know how the people of Ulster met him. If a similar abuse of power should ever occur at any future time —be it on the part of a parliament or on the part of a king—should ever occur at any future time, I do not believe that the people of Ulster have lost their sturdy love of freedom or their detestation of arbitrary power. . . . Whether the Ulstermen choose to put themselves against the rest of Ireland, whether, if they do so, they will succeed, is a matter for their consideration."—(Covent Garden, *May* 6, 1892.)]

Then we find Lord Salisbury a week later at Hastings, extending his patronage to "Fair Trade." He dare not propose to put a tax on food and raw materials, but he will put a duty on silks and gloves and hops and that sort of thing. Or, as Sir William Harcourt put it, he nibbles at Protection and mumbles the game he dare not bite :—

This list of things, better left unsaid, might be considerably enlarged, but it is large enough to explain Sir William Harcourt's description of the Prime Minister as the Malaprop of Politics :—

THE MALAPROP OF POLITICS.

XVI.—*LORD SALISBURY'S "SPIRITED FOREIGN POLICY."*

The Tories take special credit to themselves for Lord Salisbury's foreign policy, and applaud him as a great and spirited minister, who upholds British prestige in all parts of the world. But what would Lord Salisbury's supporters have said if Mr. Gladstone had hauled down the British flag as he did when he gave Heligoland to the Germans?

"HAULING DOWN THE BRITISH FLAG."

LORD SALISBURY'S FOREIGN POLICY (continued).

Or supposing Mr. Gladstone had put a portion of the British Empire up for auction, for sale, or exchange?

"THE BRITISH EMPIRE UP TO AUCTION."

LORD SALISBURY'S FOREIGN POLICY (continued).

The fact is that the merits of Lord Salisbury's foreign policy consist in the very last thing for which the Tory party can take credit: Lord Salisbury has learnt the lesson of the great Midlothian Campaign which brought his old leader to ruin, and has abjured Jingoism and all its ways. If anything, he has been too accommodating to "the foreigner," and there is some force in the drawing which depicts him as an Englishman in German uniform. Lord Salisbury, it has been said, has given Germany everything for nothing. He has (1) secured the Triple Alliance for Germany by making Italy believe that England will protect her against France. (2) He has given Germany a vast tract in Africa, to which British trade and British missionaries had penetrated, but in most of which no German had ever set foot. (3) He has made over to alien sway the loyal subjects of Her Majesty in Heligoland. The number of Heligolanders who "opted" for British nationality was small, because there was a very reasonable fear of how the German Government might behave to those who did so "opt." The apprehension was just. When the Britishers applied for their usual places in the ferry-boats—one of the most lucrative summer employments—they were told the places would only be filled by German subjects. On what principle is it that Lord Salisbury defends his alienation of a portion of the British Empire from British sovereignty, whilst, in the case of another portion thereof (Ulster), he declares that to delegate authority from the Imperial to a subordinate Parliament—within that sovereignty—would be an outrage justifying civil war?

COUNT HATFELD VON SALISBURY.

We wonder, too, whether the Persian tobacco job is to be counted another triumph of Lord Salisbury's "spirited foreign policy"? Certain speculators—a Mr. Talbot, a relative of the Prime Minister, among them—obtained, by means unspecified, a tobacco monopoly from the Shah. They then sold it to certain other Englishmen for £300,000. The Shah then revoked the concession. Whereupon the full resources of our Foreign Office are brought into line in order to obtain for a set of private speculators "compensation" for having bought a worthless bargain. The Foreign Office succeeds, with the final result that Russia offered to step in to accommodate Persia, thereby dealing a heavy and possibly a fatal blow to British influence in the country. Meanwhile, the Persian people is to be taxed in perpetuity, under pressure from Lord Salisbury, in order to compensate the concession-mongers. Is this a "foreign policy" of which any honest men can be proud?

XVII.—THE TORY HOME POLICY.

Just as they have tried to be friends at the same time with the Pope and the Orangemen, so have the Tories tried to give one hand to the Temperance party and another to the Publicans. Here is a picture of Mr. Facing-both-ways Ritchie :—

To Mr. Temperance CAINE : "Compensation, my dear sir, certainly not."
To Mr. Tory BUNG : "Compensation, my dear sir, why certainly."

THE TORY HOME POLICY (continued).

Mr. Goschen also tried to ride the two horses at once :—

But the end was disastrous.   The attempt to endow the public-house in the Local Government Bill of 1888
came wholly to grief and nearly ruined the Government :—

Yet even this did not prevent them from having another try in 1890, but that also ended disastrously for
them.

THE TORY HOME POLICY (continued).

DEAR SUGAR.

But they had another plan. They said sugar is too cheap; we must make it dearer or the sugar-refiner will lose his profits. So they held a great conference and brought in a Bill to prevent foreign nations sending us so much cheap sugar. But there was a very vigilant bird who swooped down on the Protectionist worm and saved the working-man from having to pay more for every pound of sugar :—

Yet even this did not prevent the Prime Minister from declaring that he would like to make a great many other things dearer in order to spite the foreigner. And this is what they call "Fair Trade."

THE TORY HOME POLICY (continued).

But then they say, "we are such a Radical Government." But if the water is pumped from the Radical well it tastes Tory and comes out of the "Tory spout" :—

" You will *find here* a bounteous affluence of fresh water from the Tory pump by the simple act of fitting it with a brand-new Radical handle, kindly lent for the occasion by a friend from Birmingham."—MR. JOHN MORLEY, at Leeds, *November* 1880.

Still, there was one member of the Government who made fine speeches full of Radical promises. But this is what they wanted to do with him :—

FOR THE SAFETY OF THE GOVERNMENT.
(With Apologies to Mr. E. Caldwell.)

THE TORY HOME POLICY (continued).

In short, the Radicalism of the Tories was like the vanishing lady in the music halls :—

The Tories also said they were friends of the working-man. But when it came to giving the working-man the measures which he wanted, they declined to move until compelled by the real Radicals. Here we see how Mr. Matthews was clean bowled by a Radical ball :—

[On June 18, 1891, in Committee on the "Factory and Workshops Bill," Mr. S Buxton brought forward his amendment raising the age at which children might begin to work from 10 to 11. Sir John Gorst informed the House that the English delegates at Berlin were instructed by Lord Salisbury to assent to 12 as the limit of children's labour. Nevertheless, the Government opposed the amendment, but were defeated by 202 to 186.]

50

THE TORY HOME POLICY (*continued*).

But, say the Unionists, we have carried Free Education. Yes; but, as they explained [themselves, their " sole object in taking up this question at all was to save and to promote the welfare of the Voluntary Schools " (letter from Mr. SIDNEY HERBERT to Mr. G. A. KING.)

"DON'T RIDE HIM TOO HARD."

So, when Sir William Hart-Dyke brought out his horse, "Free Education," he was told not to ride him too hard.

THE TORY HOME POLICY (continued).

Altogether the Tory policy was a mixture of hash and resurrection pie, and John Bull, who likes good food well cooked, has pulled a very wry face over it :—

" RESURRECTION PIE."

WHAT IRISH COUNTY COUNCILLORS MAY DO.

But then there is their Irish policy, which they call "triumphant." Six years ago they were going to have no Coercion, and to satisfy all the demands of Ireland by passing a Local Government Bill, which was to be on the same lines, and passed at the same time, as the Local Government Bills for England, Wales, and Scotland. They have had Coercion the whole time; they have passed no Local Government Bill at all; and they have introduced a Bill which they never meant to pass, and which is only a sort of political Aunt Sally. Mr. Balfour himself says it is not half so important as the Coercion Bill, and if it passed it would leave the Irish councillors liable to be put in the dock and condemned by two judges. Indeed, no one knows what the Irish councillors could do except kill beetles and break stones. This is their triumphant alternative policy.

MR. BALFOUR'S "AUNT SALLY."

THE FIRST STICK: MR. SEXTON.

The truth is, Lord Salisbury has been going after Liberal fruit which he can't quite reach, and is in very serious danger of losing his balance in the effort. Sometimes he goes fishing, and, though he has landed one or two big ones which came to be caught, their places are soon filled, and there are now a great many more fish in the Liberal waters than when Lord Salisbury first went out fishing :—

" The incompleteness of the Government's legislation is, in my opinion, one of its greatest recommendations. . . . If you tell me that the measure for establishing Free Education is incomplete because it does not establish popular control over all schools, I say I again rejoice that their legislation should be incomplete," &c.—(LORD HARTINGTON, at Liberal Unionist Federation, June 1891.)

XVIII.—JOSEPH THE APOSTATE.

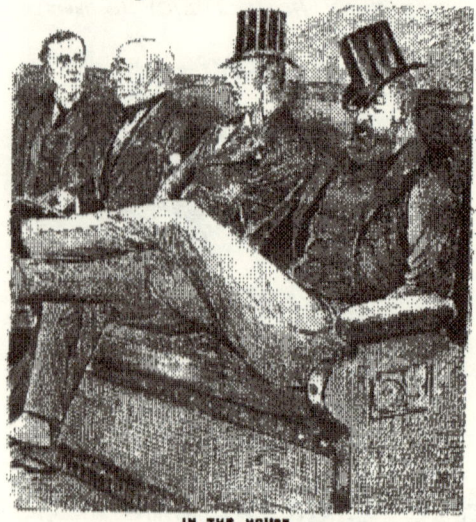

IN THE HOUSE.

A noble Marquis soliloquises :— "'No right by courtesy or custom to occupy a seat on the front opposition bench.' Quite true. Still by sitting here we crowd and worry the Old Man, and either prevent or overhear the confidential communications of the party."

AND OUT OF IT.

At least our allies will be English gentlemen."—(Mr. CHAMBERLAIN, at Birmingham, *June* 1, 1887.)

JOSEPH THE APOSTATE *(continued)*.

The double result of a change of atmosphere : —

POLITICALLY.

SOCIALLY.

JOSEPH THE APOSTATE (continued).

THE RENUNCIATION OF ST. JOSEPH.
(With Apologies to Mr. CALDERON, R.A.—From *Truth*.)

"I neither look for nor desire reunion."—Mr. CHAMBERLAIN, at Conservative luncheon, Birmingham November 1891.) The following day Mr. Chamberlain explained to an interviewer that his speech had been much misunderstood.

THE THREE JOLLY RATSMEN.

(With Apologies to the memory of RANDOLPH CALDICOTT.)

It's of three politicians, an,
a rattin' they did go;
An' they ratted, an' they
'ranted, an' they blew
their horns also.

    Look ye there !

An' one said, " Mind yo'r
een, an keep yo'r noses
reet i' th' wind,
An' then, by scent or seet,
we'll lee o' summat to
our mind."

    Look ye there

They ratted, an' they ranted,
an' the first thing they did
find
Was a Grand Old Statesman
in a field, an' him they left
behind.

    Look ye there !

One said it was a Statesman,
an' another he said, " Nay;
It's just a Liberal Party, that
has been and gone astray."

    Look ye there !

JOSEPH THE APOSTATE (*continued*).

A LESSON IN SPELLING:
R—A—N—S—O. M – PENSION.

"Society, as a whole, owes something to these veterans of industry. You see I have not altogether forgotten the doctrine of ransom, although I am very willing to confess that the word was not very well chosen to express my own meaning."—(Mr. CHAMBERLAIN, at Birmingham, *November* 1891.)

JOSEPH THE APOSTATE (continued).

SPRINGING HIS RATTLE.

JUNE 4, 1885.

"I sometimes think that great men are like great mountains, and that we do not appreciate their magnitude while we are still close to them. You have to go a distance to see which peak it is that towers above its fellows, and it may be that we shall have to put between us and Mr. Gladstone a space of time before we know how much greater he has been than any of his competitors for fame and power. I am certain that justice will be done to him in the future, and I am not less certain that there will be a signal condemnation of the men who, moved by motives of party spite, in their eagerness for office, have not hesitated to load with insult and indignity the greatest statesman of our time."

OCTOBER 21, 1891.

"I will tell you this, that, if I could consider only the interests of the party to which I belong, I would wish nothing better than that Mr. Gladstone should have the majority for which he asks, and that he should be allowed once more to show what an awful mess he would make of our affairs. . . .

"One thing I venture to predict—in six months from their (the Liberals) attaining to office, we shall once more find ourselves in those European complications which so embarrassed and baffled the last government of Mr. Gladstone. . . . Every three years they will have to go again and ask the approval of the nation upon the messes they have made."

JOSEPH THE APOSTATE (continued).

COCK OF HIS OWN WALK.

"It is very obvious why Mr. Chamberlain barred Lord Randolph out of Birmingham. It would never do to have two rival bantams on the same walk."—(Daily Paper.)

Mr. Chamberlain sworn in as Privy Councillor in 1880.
"I swear to keep the Queen's counsel secret."—(Extract from Privy Councillor's Oath.)

"After he became a minister, my principal recollection of him is that he was frequently most anxious to betray to us the secrets and counsels of his colleagues in the Cabinet."—(Mr. PARNELL, in the House of Commons, *July* 1888.)

JOSEPH'S DREAM.

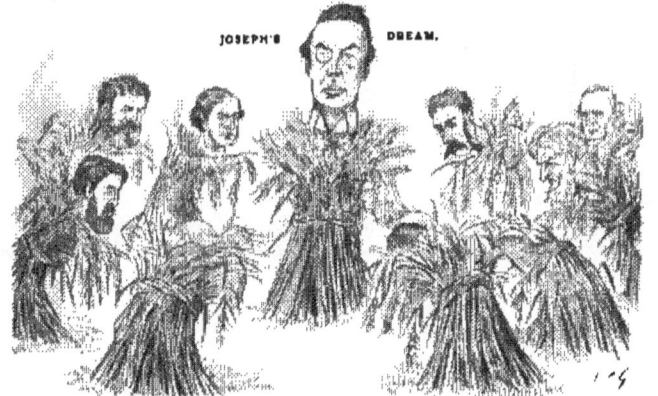

"And Joseph dreamed a dream, and he told it to his brethren. . . . And he said unto them, Hear, I pray you, this dream which I have dreamed: for, behold, we were binding sheaves in the field, and, lo, my sheaf arose, and also stood upright; and, behold, your sheaves stood round about, and made obeisance to my sheaf."—(Genesis xxxvii. 5–7.)

" Mr. Labouchere read out a list of ceremonial officers drawing large salaries. I should, he said, sweep all these away. There is no objection to people being Gold Sticks, Lords-in-Waiting, or Masters of the Buck-Hounds, if they did not cost money to the State. There are many who would be ready to take the honourable office. The Right Hon. Member for West Birmingham would, I am sure, be ready to don the uniform."—(Parliamentary Report, *August 1889*.)

JOSEPH THE APOSTATE *(continued).*

THE DOWN GRADE.

PART II.

SCENES and FACES in PARLIAMENT, 1886–92.

I.—IN THE HOUSE OF COMMONS.

THE MAJESTY OF THE HOUSE.

MR. SPEAKER.

! MR. CHAIRMAN: "ORDER, ORDER!"

At the Bar.

Admiral Field and
Mr Maclure
Cheer up my hearty!

SOME ZOOLOGICAL STUDIES.

Mr. BALFOUR : "An Irish Secretary requires the hide of a rhinoceros."

THE GRAND OLD LION   (From a Cartoon by Mr Hugh Thomson.)

A GLADSTONE EVENING.

IN REPOSE.

IN ACTION.

AWAKE.

ASLEEP.

WIDE AWAKE.

EXPOSITORY.

DECLAMATORY.

CONCILIATORY.

MINISTERS AND LEADERS.

THE LEADER OF THE HOUSE.

THE ASSISTANT LEADER OF THE
HOUSE (MR. SEXTON).

THE PRESIDENT OF THE LOCAL
GOVERNMENT BOARD.

THE HOME SECRETARY.

THE SECRETARY TO THE
TREASURY (SIR JOHN GORST).

E 2

THE TWO STYLES.

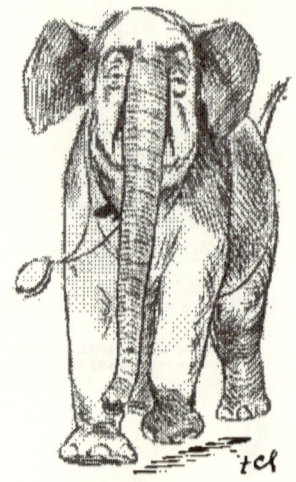

SIR W. HARCOURT IN AN ELEPHANTINE MOOD.

"IN HIS BEST WHITECHAPEL STYLE."

HODGE AND HIS
FRIENDS.

"HARCOURT'S YOUR FRIEND, NOT CHAPLIN."

"CHAPLIN'S YOUR FRIEND, NOT HARCOURT."

SCOTTISH WIT (DR. WALLACE)

"THE CAMPBELLS ARE COMING."
MESSRS. HUNTER, "EGGLEMONT," SIR G. CAMPBELL, MR. CAMPBELL-
BANNERMAN, SIR G. TREVELYAN, AND DR. CAMERON.)

A back view
in the
Lobby
Mr Radcliffe Cooke

Gallant little WALES

(MESSRS. DILLWYN, S. EVANS, LLOYD-GEORGE, AND STUART RENDEL.)

THE TWO HARCOURTS.

[SIR WILLIAM AND "LULU".

"ORCHIDES AMBO": JOSEPH AND AUSTEN

WHO'S THAT LAUGHING?

THE CULPRIT.

BIRD'S-EYE VIEW OF A LARGE HOLDING.

MR. CHAPLIN'S POLITICAL MOUNT.

AS POMPOUS AS CHAPLIN. MR. CHAPLIN AS ECCLESIASTICAL "AS HEAVY AS HARCOURT."
COMMISSIONER.

MR. H. H. FOWLER.

THE FATHER OF THE HOUSE
(MR. VILLIERS).

MR. BALFOUR.

ORLANDO FURIOSO
(MR. W. O'BRIEN).

MR. "BOB" REID:
"I CAN'T HELP LAUGHING."

"ZUR JAN" MOWBRAY.

"MILD PERSISTENCE"
(MR. STANSFELD).

Awfully slow

THE CHANCELLOR OF THE
EXCHEQUER.

THE LAST OF THE JINGOES
(MR. ASHMEAD-BARTLETT).

TEACHER CHAPLIN AND PUPIL GOSCHEN.

"Mr. Chaplin doubted if Mr. Goschen or any Member of the Government knew the difference between a horse or a cow." (That, of course, was before the Government appointed Mr. Chaplin.)

[Teacher Ch n : "Now, my little boy, can you tell me which is the cow and which the horse?"

Pupil Gos n : "Please, sir, don't know, sir."]

NURSE COLLINGS AND THE CAUCUS BABY.

"Which I nussed 'im as a baby and knows 'is tricks, and which it's only 'n old Jesse as can manage 'im—drat the little beast."

[See Mr. Jesse Collings's speech in the House of Commons, March 2, 1888 :—" His hon. friends had in the caucus a machine which they did not know how to use. He knew its tricks."- The Speaker: "The constitution of the caucus is not before the House" (laughter).- Mr. Collings : "I must confess that I have been led into a digression."]

A SKETCH BY MR. LOCKWOOD, Q.C.

NURSE COLLINGS AND THE CAUCUS BABY.

HIS ONE MISTAKE.

INTRODUCTION OF "YOUNG
HOPEFUL."

"WHICH I NUSSED MASTER
AUSTEN AS A BABY."

UNCLE DICK.

MR. CHAMBERLAIN FOR THE CHURCH.

MR. CHAMBERLAIN AND HIS SQUIRE.

CRIMINAL AND GAOLER (MR. DILLON AND MR. BALFOUR).

ON THE POUNCE.

A SUGGESTION FOR THE RE-AFFORESTING OF IRELAND.

BALFOUR THE BOUNTIFUL.

THE QUEEN'S CHRONICLER.

MR. MADDEN'S MANNAH:
A DEFENDAH OF THE BILL.

THE NEW LEADER (MR. J. REDMOND).

DIGNITY AND IMPUDENCE.

MR. T. W. RUSSELL.

COLONEL SAUNDERSON.

"LONG JOHN."
(To be continued in our next.)

MR. J. O'CONNOR.
(*Culloud.*)

"TIS A MOST DISTRESSFUL
COUNTRY."

AN AUTHORITY ON TUBERS
(MR. SWIFT McNEILL.)

MR. TIM HEALY   "YAH."   "TAY PAY": "NO VULGAR TRAMS FOR ME."   THE WRONGS OF IRELAND
MR. W. O'BRIEN.

A GOOD BUFFER (MESSRS. McCARTHY, POTTER, AND PARNELL).

GENERAL FRASER: A LOCUS STANDI.

MR. STOREY

THE NEW DUKE: A LISTENER FROM ANOTHER PLACE.

SIR CHARLES RUSSELL.

A CONSULTATION (MR. MATTHEWS AND SIR E. CLARKE).

THE ATTORNEY-GENERAL.

COUNSEL FOR THE "TIMES."

"ST. WEBSTER."

"SWEET REASONABLENESS" (MR. LABOUCHERE).

FROM THE HOUSE TO THE ABBEY; WHY NOT?

"ENJOYING THE ESTIMATES."

MR. ATHERLEY JONES.?

DR CLARK.

MR. WADDY, Q.C.

MR. J. BRUNNER.

"RANDY."

MR. COBB: "TENACITY."

"THE WORKMAN'S GUARD"
(MR. PICKERSGILL).

"THE RAILWAY SERVANTS'
FRIEND" (MR. CHANNING).

"THE CHAMPION OF THE
SWEATED" (MR. SYDNEY BUXTON).

"AT LAST!"

READY TO START.

CHAPLINUS PRÆTOR

O FORTUNATOS NIMIUM SUM SI BONA NORINT AGRICOLAS

"THE MAN IN RUSSET"
MR. GRAY).

AN INDIAN COUNCIL
(MESSRS. SWIFT, McNEILL, AND SEYMOUR KEAY,
AND SIR R. TEMPLE.

THE GRAND OLD CHARMER.

THE UNDER-SECRETARY FOR
INDIA (MR. GEORGE CURZON).

THE COMPLETE CYNIC
(SIR J. GORST).

THE COMPLETE BORE (MR.
SEYMOUR KEAY).

BAFFLED.

FERGUSSON PASHA.

MR. GOSCHEN. A SOFT ANSWER.

INSCRUTABLE.

MR. AKERS-DOUGLAS.
(After a Govt. Defeat.)

PARKS, PALACES, AND PLUNKET.

THE NEW IRISH SECRETARY
(MR. JACKSON).

LEGS (MR. BALFOUR)

FINGERS (BARON DE WORMS)

TERRIBLE EFFECTS OF THE BLACK;MAN SPEECH. (See p. 00.)

"Why, I was born in Ceylon !"   " Why, I'm a trifle dark myself !"
(Mr. MATTHEWS).   (Mr. RITCHIE).

THE HON. FRED SMITH.   EXIT MR. ATKINSON.

Rouge

Noir

"CONSTABLE PULESTON."

COLONEL KENYON-SLANEY.

MR. FORREST FULTON.

THE DAUGHTER OF THE HORSELEECH
(ADMIRALS FIELD AND MAYNE).

THE CHARGE OF THE VOLUNTEERS
(COLONELS HOWARD VINCENT
AND LAURIE).

GENERAL HAMLEY.

SIR WILFRID LAWSON.

THE STRONGER SEX (MR. SAM. SMITH).

THE LADIES' CHAMPION (SIR A. ROLLIT).

MR. CAMPBELL-BANNERMAN.

SIR LYON PLAYFAIR.

MR. DILLWYN.

THE SPINSTERS' FRIEND (MR. WYNDHAM).

MR. PICTON.

MR. MORTON: "NOT IN IT."

MR. CREMER.

MR. WINTERBOTHAM.

MR. H. LAWSON.

"ST. PANCRAS"
(MR. T. H. BOLTON).

MR. CYRIL FLOWER AND JOHN BURNS.

SIR F. S. POWELL.

MR. JIM LOWTHER AND HIS HOBBY-
HORSE.

TANGLED IN TITHES (SIR M.
HICKS-BEACH).

"BOBBY SPENCER": "NOW,
I AM NOT AN AGRICUL-
TURAL LABOURER."

SOME PARLIAMENTARY HEAVY-WEIGHTS (SIR W. HARCOURT,
SIR R. FOWLER, MR. J. W. MACLURE, AND MR. CHAPLIN).

AN INDIAN GRIEVANCE (THE SHEIK OF CAMBORNE).

DR. TANNER.

MR. CUNINGHAME GRAHAM.

MR. MORGAN: "PLEASE, SIR, HE CALLED ME SORDID."

PROFESSOR BRYCE ON ARMENIA.

MR. GEDGE.

"PETER THE PROVOST" (MR. ESSLEMONT).

"PROTESTANT" ULSTER (MR. WOLFF).

MR. H. S. KING.

MR. BALFOUR'S ATTITUDE TO THE HOUSE.

DIVISION BELL RINGS: THE HOUSE FILLING.

MR. ──── UP: THE HOUSE EMPTYING.

II.—GLIMPSES IN THE HOUSE OF LORDS.

THE WOOLSACK.

THE MARQUIS.

THE FRONT BENCH OF BISHOPS
(THE ARCHBISHOP OF CANTERBURY, THE BISHOP OF LONDON, THE LATE BISHOP OF CARLISLE,
THE BISHOPS OF WINCHESTER, SALISBURY, AND RIPON).

A WATCHING BRIEF FOR THE CHURCH
(DR. BENSON AND DR. TEMPLE).

THE FRONT OPPOSITION BENCH
(LORDS RIPON, KIMBERLEY, AND SPENCER)

KINDRED SPIRITS
(MR. ATKINSON AND LORD DENMAN).

THE EARL OF WEMYSS.

LORD KIMBERLEY.

LORD RIPON WITH HIS SCEPTRE.

A VERY SUPERIOR PERSON
(THE DUKE OF ARGYLL).

THE LATE LORD WARDEN.

BROKEN SLUMBERS.

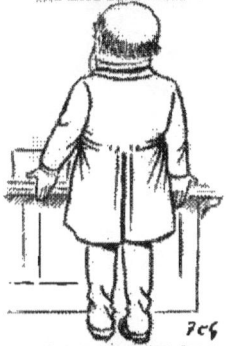

("STORY, GOD BLESS YOU, SIR, I
HAVE NONE TO TELL.")

THE HONEST BARMAN.

MR. SMITH AS SAM WELLER.
("Would any other gentleman
like to ask me anything?")

BENEVOLENCE.

MR BRADLAUGH

THE LATE MR. JOSEPH BIGGAR.
(" Mr. Courtney, sir, before the vote is taken I should like to make one or two observations.")

SIR ROBERT FOWLER.

FINIS

?OLITICAL POWDER AND SHOT.

For particulars with regard to the republication of any portions of
"HE ELECTOR'S PICTURE BOOK" in the form of Leaflets, Hand-
s, or otherwise, and for permission to use any of the Illustrations,
plication should be made to

THE MANAGER,

"Pall Mall Gazette,"

2 Northumberland Street, Strand, W.C.

☞ *For particulars of other Leaflets and Political Handbooks published by
the "PALL MALL GAZETTE," see last page of wrapper.*

Will be published immediately after the General Election,

HE POPULAR GUIDE

TO THE

NEW HOUSE OF COMMONS.

With Mems. about Members and Particulars of the Polling

◄ The former issues of this Unique and Unconventional Handbook
ained a phenomenal success. The forthcoming new issue, while pre-
ving all the distinctive characteristics of its forerunners, will contain
ny New Features and Improvements.

*Candidates will much oblige by sending their Portraits to the Editor,
the undermentioned address.*

"PALL MALL GAZETTE" OFFICE,
2 NORTHUMBERLAND STREET, STRAND, W.C.